BADJELLY. THE WITCH

a fairy story

VIKING

VIKING
An imprint of Penguin Books

Penguin Books (NZ) Ltd, cnr Rosedale and Airborne Roads, Albany,
Auckland 1310, New Zealand
Penguin Books Ltd, 27 Wrights Lane, London W8 5TZ, England
Penguin Putnam Inc, 375 Hudson Street, New York, NY 10014, United States
Penguin Books Australia Ltd, 487 Maroondah Highway, Ringwood, Australia 3134
Penguin Books Canada Ltd, 10 Alcorn Avenue, Toronto, Ontario, Canada M4V 3B2
Penguin Books (South Africa) Pty Ltd, 5 Watkins Street,
Denver Ext 4, 2094, South Africa
Penguin Books India (P) Ltd, 11, Community Centre, Panchsheel Park,
New Delhi 110 017, India

Penguin Books Ltd, Registered Offices: Harmondsworth, Middlesex, England

First published in Great Britain by M & J Hobbs
in association with Michael Joseph Ltd 1973
Puffin paperback edition first published in New Zealand by Penguin Books, 1995
First published in this form in Great Britain by Virgin Publishing Ltd, 2000
This hardback edition first published in New Zealand by Penguin Books, 2001

1 3 5 7 9 10 8 6 4 2

Printed in Spain by Bookprint, S.L., Barcelona
ISBN 0 670 91123 2

www.penguin.com

Badjelly. The Witch

a fairy story

by

Spike Milligan

Tim and Rose

To my daughter Jane
and
to Badjelly the Witch
who comes out of this worst
and to Dinboot
who is a loser

This book is written in his own handwriting by

Spike Milligan

Once upon a time, a long time ago, there was a little boy and girl. Their names were Tim and Rose. Tim was six years old, and Rose was five. Tim had black hair and blue eyes. Rose had red hair that hung down to her waist, and green eyes like the sea.

They lived with their Mummy and Daddy in a big log cabin made from wood trees, with a yellow straw roof and little birds made nests for their eggs in it. Their Daddy was a fisherman. He caught fish in a big lake near their house, their mummy used to bake lovely fresh bread for them and in the evenings, by the fire she would play the trombone for them.

They had a
fluffy cat, called
'Fluffybum', and a
white puppy-dog
called Pom-Pom
who was very
clever and could
play the piano
with his tail.
  Every morning
Tim and Rose
used to go to
Lucy their cow, to get some

FLUFFY BUM THE
CAT

POM POM

milk for their breakfast, but!
when they got to the shed
where Lucy lived, the door
was open and Lucy was gone!
So the children ran to the
field where Lucy used to eat
the grass, and shouted "Lucyyy!
Where are youuuu"! But there
was no sound of Lucy anywhere!

"Look Rose" said Tim, and he
pointed to the ground where
they could see Lucy's hoof
marks in the mud.

"Let's follow them and see where she's gone" said Rose.

They started to walk and follow the hoof marks. They walked and walked and walked.

"Are you getting tired" said Tim.

"Only my legs" said Rose.

After a long while the children came to a big forest, with very big trees, some as tall as a church, and some as thick as their teachers legs at school. There was still no sign of Lucy their cow.

"Its getting very dark-and-night-time" said Rose "We

Lucy the Cow ⒮ⓜ

better go home, or Mummy and Daddy will be worried about us". Tim said "No, we must find Lucy first, or she might get lost forever and we would never have milk on our porridge again" Rose said "Alright.
So, on they went into the great black forest, but it got so dark they could'nt see where to go.

"Are you frightened"? said
Rose.
"Only a little bit" said Tim.

"I feel very sleepy" said Rose,
"So do I" said Tim "We better
find some where to sleep".
Just then a little voice said
"You can come and sleep in

my tree".
The children looked around
but could'nt see anyone!
"Who said that"? Tim said
"I did! said the little voice.
The children looked down,
and there, standing in a little
door at the bottom of a tree
was a teeny-weeny man!
as tiny as a match stick.
He was wearing a butter-
cup yellow jacket, black
trousers with pink spots, red

shiny shoes with gold buckles and a white pointed hat with a sausage sewn on the front, with him was a green grass-hopper which the little man had on a little dogs lead."

I'm Binklebonk the Tree Goblin.

"Who are you" said the children.

I'm not. I'm a Flea.

"My name is Binkle-bonk" he said

"I'm a tree goblin. I live
in this tree, and this grass-
hopper is my guard dog, his
name is Silly-Sausage.
    Just then Silly-Sausage the grass-
hopper went "Bow-Wow Woof-Woof-"
    "What a funny grass-hopper"
said Tim "he's barking like a
doggie". Yes said Binkle-bonk
"That's why I call him Silly-
Sausage".
    Then they heard strange
noises coming from the dark
forest "Rooarr! Roooar!!"

Then "Squeak"
"What was that"! said the
children. "That" said Binkle-
bonk "That was a tin lion".
"Why did he go squeak"
asked Tim. "He's rusty from
sleeping in the rain, you'd
better come inside my tree before

he comes" said Binklebonk.
"We're too big to get in
. that, that tiny door".
"Don't worry about that"
said Binkle-bonk "I can make
the tree bigger", "You
can't", said the children.
"Oh yes I can" he
said "Watch me."
He took his finger and
he pressed a
button on his
suit and sang
this song:-

Tree Tree
One two three
Please grow very
Big for me!
And like magic, the tree got
bigger and bigger and BIGGER,
until the door was big enough
to go in.
"Follow me" said Binkle-bonk,
and they all ran inside and locked
the door. They followed Binkle-
bonk up a round and round stair
case, all the way up there were
fire flies and glow worms to

light, the darkness.

When they got to the top, there were two lovely little childrens bed-rooms, a white one with red roses for Rose and a lemon one with brown teddy bears for Tim. "Keep your windows shut to-night" said Binkle-bonk "because there are some trouser-robbers in the woods and they might rob Tims trousers, and in the morning poor Tim would have to go out without his trousers and just

his bare bottom, and if he
was'nt careful, a chicken might
peck it and make him jump
up in the air"!
Before they went
to bed, Binklebonk
gave them a real
goblins supper, some nuts, honey
and some dandelion-tea. Before
they went to sleep, the children
asked Binklebonk if he had seen
Lucy the cow go by his tree.
"Well" he said " I saw a black

and white cow go by here
this morning."

Rose said "Was she wearing
a hat"? Binkle-bonk laughed "yes,
she was wearing a straw hat,"
Tim said "Hooray! thats our Lucy"
so the children went to sleep
very happy because they knew
their cow was still alive.

During the night, there was
a terrible thunder storm with
fork lightning, knife lightning and
spoon lightning "What a funny
storm" said Tim. Out side the rain
was pouring onto the trees,

lots of birds nests got full of water and all the baby birdies were standing on the sides and diving in like a swimming pool! All the time poor old tin-lion was saying,

"Oh dear, all this rain is making me rusty, "roar-roar squeak squeak".

II

Next morning, the rain stopped, the sun came up and said "Come on, time to get up everybody. I'm going to be very good to-day, I promise I will shine all day and I won't hide behind any clouds".

Binkle-bonk came in and gave the children a cup of fresh rabbits milk, some honey and fairy cakes. When they were dressed, the children said good-bye to Binkle-bonk and went off to find Lucy the cow. "Be very careful in the forest" said a little robin from a tree "because there is a wicked witch in there, her name is BADJELLY, she catches little children and turns them into sausages and eats them! Sometimes she chops children up and makes Boy-Girl soup"!

BE VERY CAREFUL

On and on went the children
until they came to a big river with
water rushing over the rocks. The
children didn't know how to get across,
so they sat down to think how
to do it.

"Oi! mind where you're sitting boy"
said a voice from underneath Tim,
it was a little worm "You big silly,
you nearly squashed me flat like a
shoe lace". Tim said "I'm sorry worm. What
is your name"? The worm came right

out of the ground, and was wearing

a long thin shirt with drawings of red

noses on it "My name is mud-

-wiggle" said the worm.

"Did you see   a cow wearing

a straw hat"   said Rose

"Yes" said   Mud-wiggle"

she trod on   my tail, so I

pushed her   in the river!"

MUDWIGGLE

"You must be very strong"
said Tim

"I am the strongest worm in
all the world, because I eat
lots of mud"

The worm told the children
that Lucy had swum across
the river and got out the other
side, "Can you help us get across"
said Rose

"Yes" said Mudwiggle, "I'll
just put my swimming
costume on".

When he did that, he got
in the river "First I'll take
Rose, get in the river and
hold my tail"

"Which end is your tail"
asked Rose.

"Oh dear" said Mud-wiggle,
I'll wear my hat, so you will
know which end is "which" and
he put on a big red top hat
with a piece of cheese on top.

"Thats in case I meet any
hungry mice" said Mud-wiggle.
Rose got hold of his tail

and the funny worm swam
across and then went back for
Tim, but! when they were half
way across a big shark saw Tims
legs, swimming so he thought, ah! I'll
eat him up.

"Look out"! said Rose "Shark"!
The shark was just going to
bite Tim when "Wallop-Bonk-
Thud" Mud-wiggle hit the horridable
shark on his nose.
"Oh my nose! said the shark,

and swam away to
the sharks-nose hospital.
   Tim got out the river next
to Rose.

   "Good-bye children" said Mud-
wiggle and swam away. The sun
was shining very hot, and soon
the childrens clothes were nice
and dry. They saw an apple
an apple tree, so they plucked
two big juicy red ones.
   "Oh! my apples" said
tree. "I've never heard
an apple tree talk

before" said Rose, "I'm afraid
I am <u>not</u> an apple-tree, I am really
a policeman but I was turned
into an apple tree by the witch
called Badfelly, oh! boo-hoo! I want
to go back to my police-station and
my whistle. The children said they
couldn't help him
because they
couldn't do

magic," but if we see another
policeman we'll tell him where
you are and to bring your
whistle."

The children went on walking
until they came to a big big
mountain, but it had a big white
beard on.

"What a silly mountain! why has
it got a beard" said Rose, a little
mouse popped his head out of
a hole and said "He's got a beard
because hes lost his razor."

"We've never heard of a mountain with a white beard" said Tim.
"It's very old, <u>that's</u> why" said the mouse, "and <u>I'm</u> not really a mouse, I've been turned into one by Badjelly the witch". Poor little furry mouse, thought Rose "What is your name" said Tim. "My name" said the mouse "Is Dinglemouse," "What were you before the witch turned you into a mouse" said Rose. "I was a banana" said

Dingle the mouse, "So be careful, if you see **her**, run away" The children said they would hide if they saw her.

DINGLEMOUSE

"We must go and look for Lucy the cow" said the children. "Can I come with you, said Dinglemouse, and be your friend? I

have a good singing voice,
listen" and he sang:
  Fiddle-diddle dee
  I am a little flea
  I ran up daddys trousers
  And bit him on the knee!
  The children liked his singing
and said "Alright, you can come
with us, and look for Lucy."
  Tim picked up Dinglemouse
       and put him
       in his trouser
       pocket. "Its
        very dark

in here" said
Dinglemouse
"Where is
the light
switch"? Rose and Tim laughed
"Silly mouse, you don't have a light
in little boys' trouser pockets!"

So now they all set off to
find Lucy. They were climbing
up and up a big mountain, and
it was getting very cold, and it
started to snow.

"I'm freezing cold" said Rose

WHERE'S THE
LIGHTSWITCH

"I'm shivering too" said Tim "I'm nice and warm in your pocket" said Dinglemouse. Just then a voice behind them said:

"Hello children, can I help you"? Tim turned round and saw it was an old woman, dressed in black. "Dont be frighted" she said "I can make you nice and warm in a few seconds, Just get inside this nice sack, and you will be nice and warm".

The children
said "Oh thanks
old woman, we
were nearly
freezing to
death".

As soon as the children got into
the sack the old woman screamed
" Heh-Heh-Heh! got you!" she tied
the sack up tight " Heh-Heh-Heh
Im going to eat you all up,
because I am Badjelly the
baddest witch in all the world"!!!
She put the sack on her back,
jumped on her broomstick and
flew up-up-up- into the sky
     "Someone please help us"
shouted Tim. But no one could
could hear him because they
were very high in the sky.

III

The witch took the children to her castle on the top of a mountain. It was made of iron, and only the witch had the key to get in

At the gate was a huge horridable monster, his body was red and sticky, it had giant eyes as big as windows, it had sharp yellow teeth like needles, and its tongue was of fire and all its spit turned to steam! Sssss-Sss-it went.

When Badjelly ate children, she used to put them on the monsters fire-tongue

ONE OF THE DRAGONS IN THE WITCHES CASTLE.

to cook them.
The witch opened
the door,
inside was her
servant, a giant
called Dulboot. He was as big
as a house, he had purple hair,
and 10 eyes all around his
head so he could look <u>behind</u>
him! without turning round!
Badjelly told the giant
to take the sack with the
children in "Put them into a
dark room right up the top of

the prison tower, and don't
let them out of the sack".
In a deep voice the giant said
" ALRIGHT "
He carried the sack up thous
-ands of steps,
he opened a door
and he
threw the
sack with
the children
in, on the cold
stone floor and

locked the door. Poor Tim and Rose were crying, then out of Tims pocket popped Dinglemouse.

"Don't cry" he said "Ive got sharp teeth" and he started to nibble and nibble and he made a hole big enough for them to get out of the sack, Rose was crying "We'll never see our Mummy or Daddy again, to-morrow the witch will eat us with peanut butter", the sun was going down, and the room was getting very dark.

Dinglemouse suddenly said "I've got an idea! I know a big strong eagle called Jim, hes my friend, I'll go and try to get him". Dinglemouse jumped on the window ledge and climbed

DINGLEMOUSE

the ivy on the outside of the
tower down to the ground.
"Please hurry - the witch is going
to kill us in the morning" said the
children, so Dinglemouse ran
as fast as he could, he ran
so fast his tail caught fire
and he had to sit in a bucket
of water to put it out!

IIII

Back at the children's home their mummy was crying "Oh my poor children, where are they?"

Their daddy said "I've looked everywhere I think some animal in the forest must have eaten them". Poor mummy. "I'll never be able to play the trombone to them again", she said.

By now Dinglemouse had
reached the tree where Jim
the giant eagle lived Jim
was fast asleep. when he
heard Dinglemouse calling
"Help, Wake up Jim! Jim was a
beautiful eagle with brown feathers
on his body, white feathers on
on his head and a big yellow
beak and blue eyes and he
was nearly as strong as God.
"Hurry, the witch is going to
eat the children when

the sun comes up!" So Jim the
the Eagle quickly took off his
pyjamas, Dinglemouse jumped
on Jim's back and away
they flew "Faster, Faster Jim,
the sun will soon be coming up"
shouted Dinglemouse.

V

Back in their prison room the children were looking out the window.

"Can you see the eagle coming Tim" said Rose "No," said Tim. "Look" said Rose "The sun is starting to come up! And listen, I can hear the witch coming up the stairs."

"Step - step - step Im coming to get you" screamed the witch.

They could see her through the keyhole, and she had a big sharp knife!

Rose said "Look out the window 👁 I can see Jim the Eagle coming".

The witch was starting to open the door. Now Jim the Eagle flew up to the window "Quick children get on my back". But the witch was opening the door! The children were getting on Jim's back "Stop them"! screamed the

witch, but the
children were
on the mighty
eagles
back, and

<u>awayyy</u>. they flew away from
from the terrible witch.

She was so angry she screamed

"Stinkypoo to <u>all</u> of you!
she jumped on her fastest
broom stick and started to
chase after the children, and
she took a magic powder to

I'M COMING TO GET YOU

throw on the
children and
turn them
into big
black sausages.
Jim the Eagle flew
up and hid inside
a cloud, the
witch flew round
and round the cloud waiting for
Jim and the children to come
out, just then God came along,
and when he saw what the wicked
witch wanted to do to Jim and

Rose he told the witch to go away,
"No I wont" said the witch, and
tried to scratch Gods eye out,
so God pointed his finger at the
the witch and Berooom-Bang-
Spiddle-e-deee! The witch burst
like a bomb and
disappeared in smoke,

and her broom stick turned into
a sky-snake that
flew to the
moon.
When Jim
the Eagle
saw that Badjelly was dead
he flew the children back to the
witches castle to look for Lucy
"There she is" said Rose, and
there chained to the wall was
poor Lucy.
　　Quickly Jim flew down next to
her, she was so pleased to see

the children she went Moooo-
Moooo, and cried. Jim the Eagle
broke her chain with his beak,
but then the back door of the
castle opened and out came
Dulboot the giant.
   "Get away from that cow, it
belongs to me, shes my dinner" he

said, and he drew out his sword and
tried to chop the childrens heads
off but Jim grabbed the giant
by the hair while Dinglemouse
jumped on the giant, nibbled his belt
and down came the giants trousers!
"Oh help" said the giant Im showing

my bottom!" and he ran away and never came back.

"Now we're all safe" said Tim "Yes, thanks to Dinglemouse and Jim" and she gave them both a kiss. Then Jim got the children and Dinglemouse on his back then he flew up, grabbed Lucys horns in his strong claws and flew them back to their home. When their mummy and daddy saw them fly down on the back of a giant eagle, with Lucy hanging underneath, they ran inside the house and hid.

"Don't be frightened Mummy and Daddy, Jim is a kind Eagle and and saved our lives." Up popped Dinglemouse "So did I help save them too" he said.

So Mummy and Daddy came out with a big bag of Jellybabies and gave them to Jim + Dinglemouse, then they all played Ring-a-Roses, and then they blindfolded Lucy and played blind mans buff, and lived happily ever after until the next time.

The End

fifty-nine